♥ p u p p y & m e ♥

Bath Day

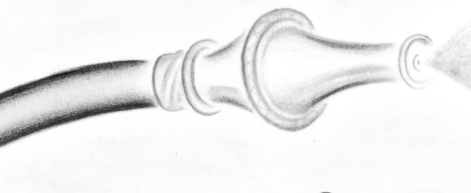

by Julia Noonan

Cartwheel BOOKS®

SCHOLASTIC INC.

New York Toronto London Auckland Sydney Mexico City New Delhi Hong Kong

My pool's warming
in the sun.
Time for doggy-
washing fun.
You'll be cleaned up
when we're done.

C'mon, Pup! It's bath day!

We get wet. The
water's cool.
We soap Puppy
in the pool.
We play doggy
beauty school.

We make waves on bath day.

I soap Puppy
up and down.
Now he wears a
bubble crown.
And a fancy,
soapy gown.

We dance 'round on bath day.

I spray Puppy
with the hose.
Wash away his
soapy clothes.
He gets water
up his nose.

Puppy shakes on bath day.

Puppy runs, and
I run, too.
Mommy says, "Come
back, you two!"
That's not what we
want to do.

We run wild on bath day.

In the dirt we
roll around.
Then we slide on
soggy ground.
Jump to make a
squishy sound!

We make mud on bath day.

Mommy sprays me
and my Pup.
When we're clean
he licks me up.
When I squeeze him
he barks "Yup!"

We're all clean on bath day.

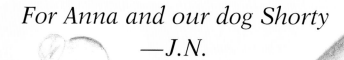

For Anna and our dog Shorty
—J.N.

Copyright © 2000 by Julia Noonan.
All rights reserved. Published by Scholastic Inc.
SCHOLASTIC, CARTWHEEL BOOKS and associated logos are trademarks and/or registered trademarks of Scholastic Inc.

12 11 10 9 8 7 6 5 4 3 2 1   0/0 01 02 03 04 05
Printed in Malaysia 46
First printing, June 2000

When it was time to go home, Mokey picked up her tired friend and carried her all the way back home. She carried her past the den of the Gagtoothed Groan, through the Falling Rock Zone, over the Great Gorge, and past the Cavern of the Creeping Crocus. "If it hadn't been for you, Red, I would never have made it to Brushplant Cave," said Mokey.

"Don't worry, Mokey," Red yawned bravely, "I'll always protect you."

"After all, what are best friends for?"